YOU CHOOSE

CAN YOU CATCH
THE KRAKEN?

AN INTERACTIVE MONSTER HUNT

BY BRANDON TERRELL

CAPSTONE PRESS
a capstone imprint

Published by Capstone Press, an imprint of Capstone.
1710 Roe Crest Drive
North Mankato, Minnesota 56003
capstonepub.com

Library of Congress Cataloging-in-Publication Data
Names: Terrell, Brandon, 1978–2021 author.
Title: Can you catch the kraken? : an interactive monster hunt / by Brandon Terrell
Description: North Mankato, Minnesota : Capstone Press, [2022] | Series: You choose : monster hunter | Includes bibliographical references and index. | Audience: Ages 8–11 | Audience: Grades 4–6
Identifiers: LCCN 2021008499 (print) | LCCN 2021008500 (ebook) | ISBN 9781663907639 (hardcover) | ISBN 9781663920300 (paperback) | ISBN 9781663907608 (ebook PDF)
Subjects: LCSH: Kraken—Juvenile literature.
Classification: LCC QL89.2.K73 T47 2022 (print) | LCC QL89.2.K73 (ebook) | DDC 001.944—dc23
LC record available at https://lccn.loc.gov/2021008499
LC ebook record available at https://lccn.loc.gov/2021008500

Summary: Reports pour in from around the world. A giant kraken lurks off the coast of Norway. A huge, snakelike sea serpent is spotted in the Mediterranean Sea. And the biggest shark ever seen reportedly roams the Pacific Ocean. Are these creatures the legendary sea monsters of old? It's up to YOU to find out! With dozens of choices, you can follow the clues to the end. Which path will YOU CHOOSE to discover the truth?

Editorial Credits
Editor: Aaron Sautter; Designer: Bobbie Nuytten; Media Researcher: Kelly Garvin; Production Specialist: Katy LaVigne

Photo Credits
Getty Images: duncan1890, 36; Jon Hughes, 72; Shutterstock: 80's Child, top 10-11, Airin. dizain, bottom 107; Bottom of Form, Al McGlashan, 48, Andrea Izzotti, 24, blue-sea.cz, 81, cgterminal, 61, Dabarti CGI, 35, David Hyde, 55, Dotted Yeti, 53, Drew McArthur, 6, Dudarev Mikhail, 99, E.A.stasy, cover, IADA, middle 106, middle left 107, Ingrid Pakats, 12, Jan Hendrik, 42, littlesam, 29, Morphart Creation, 102, Pisit Rapitpunt, 46, Sammy33, bottom 106, Shane Gross, 88, The Mariner 4291, 75, Thomas Sandberg, bottom 107, tristan tan, top 107, Umomos, 67, VisionDive, 79, W. Scott McGill, 97, zaferkizilkaya, 84

TABLE OF CONTENTS

ABOUT YOUR ADVENTURE

YOU are an oceanographer who studies and photographs marine life. You also have a strong interest in old tales about the kraken and other sea monsters. When you hear about sightings of these creatures, you're excited at the idea of finding them and getting proof of their existence. Will you be able to track down the legendary creatures?

Chapter One sets the scene. Then you choose which path to read. Follow the directions at the bottom of the page as you read the stories. The decisions you make will change your outcome. After you finish one path, go back and read the others for new perspectives and more adventures!

Turn the page to begin your adventure.

Puffer fish often make their homes in coral reefs.

CHAPTER 1

SEA CREATURE SEARCH

Splash!

You dive into the crisp, crystal-blue water of the Caribbean Sea. All around you the sea teems with life, and you capture it all with your underwater camera. A stingray slides along the ocean floor. A group of jellyfish and a spiky puffer fish float nearby.

You can't believe you get to take photos of such amazing sea creatures for your job. Today your work has brought you to a reef system in the Caribbean Sea near the coast of Jamaica. You're searching for a group, or shiver, of hammerhead sharks, and find them circling the coral reef.

Turn the page.

The sharks are a smaller variety and aren't aggressive toward humans. Still, you keep your distance as you snap a series of photos.

After a time, you swim toward the surface. Your scuba tank is nearly out of oxygen, and you have what you need for the day.

You break the surface, peel out your mouthpiece, and take a deep breath of fresh air. A large boat is anchored nearby. As you swim toward it, a man emerges from the boat's helm. His shaggy brown hair is pinned atop his head.

"Welcome back," he says with a wide smile as you climb aboard.

The man is your assistant, Mattius. He helps you shrug the scuba tank from your back.

"Did you find the sharks?" Mattius asks.

You nod.

"See any scary monsters?" he laughs. Mattius is aware of your other passion, cryptozoology. It is the study of creatures whose existence hasn't been proven, such as Bigfoot or the Loch Ness Monster.

"Not today," you reply. "Why do you ask?"

"While you were down there, I saw an article online from Norway." Mattius replies. "A fishing boat captain claims to have seen gigantic tentacles reaching up out of the ocean."

Mattius's words grab your attention. Suddenly, the beauty of the Caribbean is lost on you. You wish to know more about the sighting.

That evening in your hotel room, you decide to look up the article Mattius mentioned on your computer.

"It was like nothing I'd ever seen before," the ship's captain says in the story. "It looked like the arms of a kraken!"

Turn the page.

Tales of the kraken describe the legendary beast as a gigantic squid or octopus-like creature.

"Kraken . . ." you whisper quietly.

The kraken is a legendary cephalopod once thought to terrorize ships in ancient times. But the giant creature's existence has never been proven.

But the event in Norway isn't the only report of a mysterious sighting. You find another article about fishermen who may have spied a mythical sea serpent in the Mediterranean Sea.

Another story covers a team of great white shark trackers. They claim to have evidence near China of the largest shark ever spotted in the world. Could it be the extinct megalodon?

All of these reports sound appealing. Which creature do you want to track down?

To search for the kraken, turn to page 13.

To look for the sea serpent, turn to page 37.

To hunt down the megalodon, turn to page 73.

Ancient sailors often imagined that dangerous creatures lurked in the sea off the coast of Norway.

CHAPTER 2
THE KRAKEN OF NORWAY!

The next morning as you prepare the boat for another day at sea, you tell Mattius you're heading off to Norway.

"You are?"

"I read that article you mentioned yesterday."

"The one about the kraken?" Mattius laughs. He doesn't have the same interest in cryptid creatures that you do.

"The very one," you reply. "I'm going to try to get some photographs of the creature."

"Then I wish you the best of luck," Mattius says.

That evening after you and Mattius bring in the boat, you pack your things and prepare for a long plane ride.

Turn the page.

The following morning, you board a nearly full flight from Kingston, Jamaica, to Oslo, Norway. You're headed from the heat and sunshine of the Caribbean to the icy-cold Nordic north.

On the plane you read more about the mythical kraken. The creature was first popularized in old Norse sagas, or epic tales and poems about heroic characters. Later, sailors often drew pictures of the beast with its tentacles wrapped around large ships. Ancient tales about the kraken often describe its unspeakable size.

You also learn that ancient sailors likely mistook giant squids to be the legendary beast. You wonder just what the sailors in Norway saw, and you're anxious to hear their story.

Once you arrive in Oslo, you take a small plane to the port city where the fishing ship is docked. The docks are filled with crates of fresh seafood and people bundled up against the chilly wind.

You wander about, searching for the fishing boat. According to the article, the boat's name is *Valhalla*. It's named after the enormous hall found in Asgard, the home of the Norse gods. After a time, you find the fishing boat. Its name is painted in blue on the white hull.

As you approach, a muscular man with a thick beard appears wearing a blue beanie cap. He exits the ship and steps on the dock in front of you.

"Can I help you?" he asks in a gruff voice.

You introduce yourself and tell him you've come to find out more about the reported creature.

"Hmm. Name's Sven Olmansen." Sven thrusts out a rough hand for you to shake.

Turn the page.

"You've got the right boat. We're about to take it out for the night," Sven explains. "You're welcome to join us."

"Right now? Uh, sure . . . that would be great," you reply.

As the small crew of the *Valhalla* prepares to leave port, Sven is quite talkative. He shares all the details of the crew's creature sighting as he guides the ship out of port and steers toward the North Sea.

"There's two ways we can go," Sven explains. "We can play it safe and stay in the inlet over there. Or we can head for more treacherous waters. What say you?"

To steer toward the small inlet, go to page 17.

To head for open waters, turn to page 21.

You nod in the direction of the small inlet.

"Now, keep in mind," Sven says. "This ain't where we come across the beast. But it's an okay place to search."

"I think it's best to stay out of the more dangerous area," you explain. "That way, if we see anything, it'll be easier to get good photographs."

You remove your camera from its case as Sven turns the ship portside. The *Valhalla* slides left into the small inlet where the water is smoother.

After a while, the ocean burns bright orange and red as the sun sets across the water. Soon only moonlight will guide the ship across the waves. You can feel the excitement building as the boat glides across the smooth water.

An hour later, darkness has fallen. It's been two hours since leaving port. You haven't seen a hint of anything under the water's surface.

Turn the page.

But suddenly, as you scan the water's surface, you see a shadow pass by.

"Wait!" You wave to Sven to kill the boat's engine and point to the water. "Over there!"

As you raise your camera, another crew member turns on a large spotlight and points it at the water. Again, the shadow passes. Only this time it appears to slip under the boat. If you hadn't been in shallow waters, you may have missed it. You switch your camera over to record high-quality video.

"She's near!" Sven shouts. "Should I follow it? Or head to deeper waters?"

To follow the shadow, go to page 19.
To continue on to deeper waters, turn to page 20.

"Follow that shape!" you direct the captain.

Sven turns the ship even further to port, heading into the shallows. The spotlight catches the shadow again. But the shadow is swallowed in darkness just as you hit "record" on the camera.

You've lost sight of the shadow. As Sven brings the ship around, you hear a sickening scrape, and the boat lurches.

"What's happened?" you shout.

"Rocks!" Sven replies. "The hull caught a sharp one. Sorry, friend, but your search for the kraken is over. We gotta head back to port. *Now.*"

Your spirits sink in defeat. Your chances of finding the shadow again are slim to none. This isn't how you hoped your adventure would end.

THE END
To read another adventure, turn to page 11.
To learn more about the kraken, turn to page 103.

You watch the water for the shape to return. The crew member manning the spotlight shines it out across the inky blackness of water. Small slivers of moonlight make the water twinkle and shine.

"There!" You point again as the shape cruises under the ship. You grab the ship's railing and brace yourself. You can't help but think about images from old books that show powerful tentacles wrapped around a ship and dragging it under.

But the shape quickly disappears.

"Head for deeper water!" you direct Sven. The shape seemed to be swimming in that direction.

Sven twists the ship's wheel, and the *Valhalla* heads away from the inlet.

Turn to page 22.

"It may be easier to see the creature from shallow waters," you tell Sven. "But I think we'll have the best chance of finding the creature in deeper water."

"Good call," Sven says. He steers the craft toward the beautiful sunset of orange and red.

The deep water is choppy, and for a time even an experienced oceanographer like yourself feels a bit queasy. Your stomach settles as the sun dips below the horizon and darkness descends on you.

"Fire up the spotlight!" Sven orders. A crew member on the main deck flips the switch on a large light. Then he begins scanning the black waves for motion.

Turn the page.

The *Valhalla* bobs and shifts in the rough night waters. You have your camera at the ready. But a long time passes, and you see nothing.

However, just as you're about to ask Sven to turn around . . .

"There!" You shout and point.

The crewman swings the spotlight to where you pointed. A large shape swiftly passes through the light. When the shadow is caught in the light's glare, you snap off some photos.

Click! Ca-click!

It's not enough. You want to get closer. You've brought your scuba gear with you aboard the boat. You also have an underwater light. Do you dare go into the water with the large shape looming near?

To go into the water, go to page 23.
To remain on the boat, turn to page 30.

You've already come this far. You know that if you want to capture good images of the beast, you'll need to get into the water.

"Sven," you say to the captain, "I'm going in."

"Do you think it's safe?"

"I've done it before. I'll be fine."

You put on your scuba gear and ready your underwater camera. With the crew's help, you safely splash into the sea.

You've never grown used to being underwater at night. It's pure blackness. You click on the light attached to your gear. A steady beam makes the area around you suddenly glow bright.

Small fish scurry away from you. There's no sign of the large shape you saw earlier. You hope it didn't slip away as you were putting on your scuba gear.

Turn the page.

You decide to explore the area around you. The sea floor is deep, and there appears to be a crevasse carving its way across it. There's also a ridge of rock jutting out of the darkness.

Whoosh!

Divers must use extreme caution when exploring the dark ocean floor.

Something large swims overhead. You crane your neck to see, casting the area in light. Could it be the mysterious shape from earlier?

You try to get a fix on the location of the shape but cannot. You swing the light back and forth, but you see nothing besides fish and other typical ocean life. Certainly nothing that would make spectacular photos.

But the shape *must* be nearby.

You look around, and your eyes land on the crevasse in the ocean floor. Then you see the rocky ridge. Either would be a good place for a large creature to slip off to. But you can only explore one.

To go to the rocks, turn to page 26.
To go toward the crevasse, turn to page 28.

The rocky ridge has openings wide enough for a large creature to hide. You direct your beam of light at them. But you see nothing.

You'll have to get closer.

You swim toward the rock, scaring away a small octopus on the sea floor. It stirs up a plume of silt as it disappears. Other than that, there is very little sign of life.

The holes in the rock are large enough for you to swim through. You swim into one and cast your light in front of you.

Nothing.

You turn back to head out of the rocks when something darts out at you.

It's a shark! You quickly stop and drop your camera in surprise.

The shark wants nothing to do with you, though. It quickly swims back into the rocks. You wonder why . . .

But then a huge tentacle suddenly grabs you from behind!

Something has emerged from the crevasse behind you. Something big! Its shadow in the water is enormous! Its powerful tentacle smashes your light, leaving you in total darkness.

You swim for the surface. At least you hope it's the surface. It's your only chance at survival. Unfortunately, as you swim frantically, another tentacle snakes its way around your ankle. It pulls you back down to the ocean's depths.

There's no escape for you!

THE END

To read another adventure, turn to page 11.
To learn more about the kraken, turn to page 103.

The rocks are closer, but the crevasse is too tempting. Who knows how deep it leads? You won't need to find out, though. As you swim near, your light catches a huge tentacle in the dark!

Click! Click! Click!

You snap numerous photos of the tentacle. Your heart races, hoping the beast within the crevasse will fully appear.

The tentacle waves about. It slips along the sea floor as if searching for the source of your light.

Come on, you think, snapping more images. *Swim out just a little more.*

Unfortunately, the creature does not. Fearing the thick tentacle may reach out and grab you, you swim back to the *Valhalla*. Crew members help you climb onto the ship, and you peel the scuba mask from your face.

"I saw something!" you report as Sven joins you.

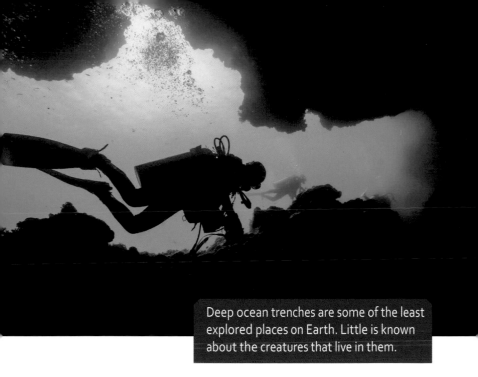

Deep ocean trenches are some of the least explored places on Earth. Little is known about the creatures that live in them.

You show him the photos. They aren't entirely clear, but the shape of the tentacle is there. It's hard to determine the size of it, though.

Still, although you can't tell exactly how large the creature was, you consider your trip to Norway a rousing success!

THE END

To read another adventure, turn to page 11.
To learn more about the kraken, turn to page 103.

You have your scuba gear. But going into the water alone at night is a dangerous and possibly deadly move. You decide to remain on the boat with the video camera instead. You hope you can record something from the deck of the *Valhalla*.

As the night goes on, though, nothing appears. Sven comes to stand near you.

"Quiet night out here," he says.

"Yes, sadly, it is," you reply.

"We've got some spoiled fish in the cargo hold," the captain suggests. "Perhaps a bit of bait will stir the waters."

You think it over. You also have a special lure with your gear. It simulates a bioluminescent glow. Both seem like a good way to lure any large creatures to the water's surface.

To use the bait, go to page 31.
To use the lure, turn to page 34.

You look out at the black water and the beam of light shining on the surface. Nothing.

Squid typically eat fish, crabs, or even other squid. Maybe Sven's spoiled fish will be the perfect lure for any large squid nearby. Or maybe even a kraken!

You nod at Sven. "Let's try that bait of yours," you say.

He nods, then tells a crewman to retrieve the spoiled fish.

You can smell the fish before you can see it. The crewman, with his nose wrinkled, quickly ties it to a line and tosses it into the water.

For a while, the lure just bobs in the water. You train a spotlight on it. Then, you see something swimming around the bait.

"There!" You point to the shape.

Turn the page.

"Aye, I see it," Sven says, turning the boat. You begin moving toward the shape slithering beneath the surface. It's big, and you're not sure what it is. You lean close to get a better look, grabbing your camera and pointing it in the shape's direction.

WHAM!

The large shape crashes against the side of the *Valhalla*. The blow causes you to drop the camera and grab for the railing. The camera teeters on the edge of the boat.

You lean over to grab it when . . .

WHAM!

Another blow strikes the boat. You're knocked overboard!

You splash into the cold water. The shock of it takes your breath away as you go under.

When you come to the surface, you hear a distant crewman holler, "Man overboard!" The spotlight searches for you back and forth across the water.

You flail about to get their attention. "Over here!" you shout.

But you feel something brush against your leg—something big. You feel it begin to wrap around your body.

"Hurry! Help!" You kick at the creature, but it's stronger than a boa constrictor. Just as the spotlight turns in your direction, it tugs you hard. You are pulled under the waves for good. You'll never get to tell the story of your encounter with the legendary kraken.

THE END

To read another adventure, turn to page 11.
To learn more about the kraken, turn to page 103.

You consider Sven's bait. Squid typically eat fish, crabs, and even other squid. Using the fish as a lure could work. But you brought the bioluminescent lure along for just this situation.

This would be the perfect time to use it, you think.

"I have an idea," you say. "One that won't make the whole ship smell like spoiled fish."

"Ha!" Sven chuckles. "Then let me help you."

Sven goes with you to get the lure. "I read about a scientist who photographed a giant squid using a bioluminescent lure," you explain. "My team purchased one, and it could be perfect for this occasion."

You remove the lure from its case and set it on the ship's deck. It's large, but you and Sven tie it to a thick rope and slide it into the water with a splash.

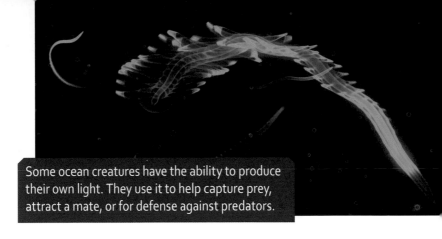

Some ocean creatures have the ability to produce their own light. They use it to help capture prey, attract a mate, or for defense against predators.

The lure glows a vibrant blue in the blackness of the sea. It's almost magical.

Soon enough, something swims near the side of the boat. You hit "record" on your camera and capture amazing footage of a large, tentacled creature. It is a giant squid, larger than any you've ever seen. It isn't the kraken of ancient lore, but it's still an amazing sight. Few people have seen a giant squid this close.

The entire crew of the *Valhalla* watches the amazing beast in awe.

THE END

To read another adventure, turn to page 11.
To learn more about the kraken, turn to page 103.

Ancient sailors often described seeing huge, snakelike creatures that they called sea serpents during their voyages.

CHAPTER 3

THE MEDITERRANEAN SEA SERPENT

"Hmm, a sea serpent," you say. "What a fascinating thing to try to track down."

It's been ages since you've traveled overseas. You decide that now is a good time to change that. You've always wanted to visit the Mediterranean Sea.

After buying your plane ticket, you read up on the mythical creature. Sightings of sea serpents have been reported for hundreds of years. According to legend, the creatures are often found near many coastal countries. Though not common, reports of the beasts continue even today.

Turn the page.

Cryptozoologists have suggested that sea serpents are actually plesiosaurs or some other reptiles from the Mesozoic era. But that seems unlikely. You keep reading and learn that sea serpents are commonly mistaken for a large, long fish known as an oarfish.

Your travels lead you to the port city of Perama in Greece. It's a beautiful, crisp sunny day when you arrive. The Mediterranean Sea glistens in an almost otherworldly blue. It's easy to imagine mythical creatures swimming in its depths.

As you explore the city, you stop at a street vendor for some *souvlaki*. The delicious grilled meat wrapped in a pita makes a perfect lunch. Children dash back and forth down the streets, and fishermen line the docks. You spy a sign reading "Boat Rentals" next to a small shack on the dock. It's just what you were looking for.

As you approach the shack, a burly man exits the shack. He looks you up and down. "How can I help you, stranger?" he asks.

You explain your desire to search for the reported sea serpent. The man listens closely, stroking his thick black beard. Then he thrusts out a hand. "Name's Stavros," he says. "You're in luck. I've got just the boat for you, serpent seeker."

Stavros seems interested in your mission. As he takes you to his boat, he says, "You know, I've got the day free. Any interest in taking on a companion for a small fee?"

You think it through. You can manage your equipment yourself. But having a guide that knows the waters could be very useful.

To simply rent a boat, turn to page 40.
To ask Stavros to join you, turn to page 51.

Having someone along that knows the area would help. But you're a skilled oceanographer, and you know your way around a boat.

"Thanks for the offer," you tell Stavros, "but I should be able to manage on my own."

"Suit yourself, friend," Stavros replies.

He leads you to a small vessel near the rental shack. The boat is a faded blue, with a worn deck and a small galley. "It's not much," Stavros says, "but it'll serve you well out on the sea."

"Thanks, Stavros," you say. You hoist your case full of gear onto the boat's deck and pay Stavros the rental fee.

"Be mindful of the wind," Stavros says. "It could get choppy out there."

You hadn't noticed, but the wind has picked up. There are whitecaps on the waves outside Perama. Still, it's nothing you can't manage.

With a wave to Stavros, you fire up the boat's engine and steer it safely from the docks. Before long, you're out in the open water of the Mediterranean Sea. The salty wind brushes against your face.

Stavros was right, though. The whitecaps are making the waters rough. Waves begin to crash against the side of the boat, spilling onto the deck. It will be difficult to navigate the ship *and* try to capture images of the sea serpent.

You cross the deck to your case of gear and remove your camera and tripod. You try to get sample photos of the water, just in case the creature appears.

WHAM!

A strong wave strikes the side of the boat. You stagger to the side and grab the railing for support.

Maybe this is too dangerous, you think.

Turn the page.

Large ocean waves can make navigating a boat or ship difficult.

The water looks calmer near the coast by Perama. You could steer the small boat portside toward the shore. Or you could steer starboard and head into deeper waters. The waves may even out there.

To steer toward the shoreline, go to page 43.

To steer into deeper waters, turn to page 45.

This may be too rough to do on my own, you think. Perhaps if you steer back toward Perama, you can find Stavros. He may still be interested in joining you.

Securing your camera, you hurry back along the slick deck to the helm. There, you twist the wheel to head back toward the shoreline. But as you turn the boat, it shifts directly into the waves.

CRASH!

Water spills over the boat, covering the deck in water. But you don't worry yet. You've experienced ocean waves far larger and more powerful than these. Besides, you'll soon be back along the safe shores of Perama.

CRASH!

Another wave splashes across the deck, jerking the wheel in your hands. Then you hear a sickening crunch that makes the boat tremble.

Turn the page.

"Oh no!" you shout. "I've struck something!"

You don't have to look below deck to know what happened. The boat has hit hidden rocks, and you're taking on water!

You need to steer the boat back to shore fast—before it sinks. Unfortunately, your mission to capture photos of the sea serpent is over before it truly began.

THE END

To read another adventure, turn to page 11.
To learn more about sea serpents, turn to page 103.

You've navigated harsh seas before. You know that if you head to deeper water, the waves could die down. You turn the wheel and steer the boat to open water.

SPLASH!

A heavy wave crashes against the side of the boat, tipping you back and forth. Water spills across the deck. Still, you fight against the waves.

After a time, the waves finally die down. Although the sea is still rough, the water is calm enough to manage the boat safely.

With the boat under control, you set up the camera and begin searching for the sea serpent.

After a while, you notice something moving in the distance. Your heartbeat quickens as a shape emerges from the water. As it surfaces, it looks like it has a spiky spine. Could it be a sea serpent? The creature is too far away to tell.

Turn the page.

Ancient sailors may have mistaken humpback whales to be serpentlike creatures when they surfaced for air.

How can I draw it closer? you wonder.

You check the boat's small hold. There you find that Stavros has left a bucket of chum, or bits of dead fish. If you pour it into the water, you may get the creature's attention.

To pour the chum into the water, go to page 47.

To go without the chum, turn to page 49.

You really want to get good photos of the creature. The stinky chum bucket may be just the thing needed to draw it closer to the boat. You grab the dented bucket and wrinkle your nose in disgust.

You head to the boat's deck and pour the bucket into the water with a sickening slop. The bloody remains stir in the waves. You toss the bucket aside with a clatter and ready your camera. There's no way you want to miss this!

Soon there's movement within the chum. Something snaps at the bits of dead fish. But it's not the creature you saw before—it's a shark.

WHAM!

As you watch the shark, the large creature strikes the side of the boat!

"Whoa!" You try to grab the boat's railing, but it's slick with water, and you can't get a grasp.

Turn the page.

Sharks can smell blood from a long distance. When chum is dumped into the ocean, it will quickly attract nearby sharks.

You tumble overboard and hit the water with a loud splash. Quickly, you swim for the boat's small ladder. But just before you reach it, you feel a tug at your leg. The shark isn't alone. The chum in the water has drawn several more sharks. They're in a feeding frenzy, with you in the middle!

Sadly for you, you'll never learn what the creature was that you saw in the distance.

THE END

To read another adventure, turn to page 11.
To learn more about sea serpents, turn to page 103.

You consider using the chum bucket. But you know it could attract the wrong kind of animals. You decide to leave the bloody bits of dead fish in the boat's hold.

You head back to the boat deck and brace yourself with your camera. Soon, evening draws near, and the sky begins to grow dark. You hope the creature returns before it's too late and you must turn back.

A few minutes later, the spiny shape breaks the surface to your left. You quickly swing the camera in that direction.

Click! Click!

You excitedly snap off several shots of a spiny hump before it's swallowed by the sea.

"Got it!" you shout into the wind, pumping your fist in excitement.

Turn the page.

"How was your adventure, friend?" Stavros asks with a smile as you pull the boat back into port.

You toss him a thick rope, and he ties the boat to the dock. "I think I have what I was looking for," you tell him.

You head back to your hotel, tired but excited from your day's search. You scroll through the images on your camera and find some good shots of the shape coming out of the water. Its spiky spine is visible and not as blurry as you imagined. It seems that you've caught evidence of—something. You can't wait to share it with the world!

THE END

To read another adventure, turn to page 11.
To learn more about sea serpents, turn to page 103.

"What do you say, friend?" Stavros asks with a smile. "I can steer the boat while you focus on your task."

As an oceanographer, you've traveled alone before. You know your way around a boat. But having an extra hand on board could be helpful.

"Sure," you reply. "Why not?"

Stavros laughs. "Good! Very good!"

He leads you to a small vessel near the rental shack. The boat is a faded blue, with a worn deck and a small galley. There, he takes your case from you and hoists it onto the boat's deck.

"Let's be off!" he says, heading for the boat's wheel.

As Stavros fires up the boat's engine, you untie the boat from the dock. Stavros then steers the boat away and heads out into open water.

Turn the page.

"You will be glad to have me along," he says. "The waters will be rough today!"

He's right. The water has grown choppy, but your captain knows exactly how to manage the waves. Even as water crashes against the boat and spills across the deck, you easily set up your camera and tripod to capture images and video.

When you've reached deep waters, the rough waves calm, and it's easier to see into the depths. You and Stavros spend the afternoon with your eyes on the sea.

"This serpent of yours, are you sure it's not just an oarfish?" Stavros asks.

"Most likely," you reply. "But cryptozoologists are always ready to believe."

"Then start believing, friend!" Stavros points across the starboard bow.

Giant oarfish can grow more than 50 feet (15 meters) long. It's easy to see how sailors might have mistaken them for sea serpents.

A short distance away, a large shadow slithers near the surface of the water. You quickly snap a few photos.

"Should we pursue it?" Stavros asks. "I fear we would scare it away."

It's a good question. You want to get great shots of the creature. But at what risk?

To follow the shape, turn to page 54.

To stay where you are, turn to page 66.

You want to get closer to the shadow. You're so excited that you bellow out, "Follow away, captain!"

Stavros turns the boat toward the shape and speeds up while you ready your camera. You get a few photos, but then the shape is swallowed by the sea.

"It's gone!" you shout.

"As I feared," Stavros says, and joins you on the deck. Together you search for the shape.

You spend most of the day looking for the shadowy shape but have no luck. As the sun is about to set, Stavros asks, "Well friend, the time grows late. Should we stay out here? Or head back to land?"

To stay past nightfall, go to page 55.
To head back to shore, turn to page 57.

It's a hard decision. The later you stay out, the harder it will be to see anything in the water. But you're not ready to give up yet.

"Let's stay out a while longer," you decide.

You stand alongside your camera, ready to get any images you can. You wait a long time, but there is nothing. The wind starts to blow stronger, and there is a chill in the air. The water begins to grow choppy again. Stavros has a small spotlight on the boat. He turns it on and scans the water with it.

Turn the page.

Small fishing boat pilots need a lot of skill to navigate on rough waters.

"There!" he shouts. His keen eye has found a shape in the water.

You see the shadowy shape, but just barely. Stavros tracks it with his spotlight, and you snap some images. The creature breaches the surface, and you can see the spiny ridge of its back. It appears to be a massive oarfish. Or could it be the legendary sea creature you've been searching for?

You bring the camera to your eye. It's hard to see the beast in the view screen.

"I need a better view," you say to yourself.

The boat has a small area above the helm with a rail. A small ladder leads up to it.

To climb the ladder for a better view, turn to page 62.
To stay on the main deck, turn to page 64.

You consider the blustery wind and choppy waves. With night coming on fast, the darkness could put you in danger. "Perhaps it's best if we call it a day," you suggest.

"As you wish," Stavros says. He begins to turn the small boat around.

That's when you see the shape in the water. It glides along the port side of the boat and swims off into the distance.

"Wait a second!" You point at the shape. "I'd like to get some video footage of it!" You grab your camera.

"Should I follow it?" Stavros asks.

To follow the shape, turn to page 58.
To set up your video camera, turn to page 60.

You consider the options, then nod your head. "Let's follow it," you say, clutching your camera.

Waves crash against the side of the boat as the waters grow even rougher. Stavros does his best to turn the boat in the direction of the shape. Meanwhile, you angle the spotlight to get a view of the creature.

It's still there, swimming to port. You hit "record" on the camera and hope the footage isn't too blurry or grainy.

"Heads up!" Stavros cries out, and a spray of water spills over the deck, dousing you.

KRNNCH!

Suddenly, there is a sickening crunch, and the boat lurches to one side. Then you notice the rocks that Stavros has accidentally steered the boat into. Your recording is forgotten as you drop the camera to hang on to the railing.

You hear a bubbling sound from the small cargo hold beneath you. When you check it, you spot a hole in the hull. Sea water is gushing in.

"We're taking on water!" you call out.

"Then we're headed for shore!" Stavros does his best to control the boat. "Sorry your mission is at an end, friend. But our lives are more important."

You scoop up the camera and check the footage. Unfortunately, it's blurry and doesn't show much. It's a disappointment, but there are more important things to consider right now. Mainly, making it to shore before the boat sinks!

THE END

To read another adventure, turn to page 11.
To learn more about sea serpents, turn to page 103.

The waves are growing in size, and steering away now could be dangerous. You shake your head. "Don't follow it," you say. "I'll set up my camera here. Maybe we can get some solid video of it."

"Sounds good to me!" Stavros calls down.

Water crashes over the side of the deck, dousing your boots. You stagger to the railing, where you've set up your tripod. You latch the camera onto it and hit "record."

The tripod wobbles, but you've secured it to the deck as best you can. With the camera set, you do your best to find the shape with the spotlight. Unfortunately, the shape in the water appears to have vanished.

Maybe following it would have been the better option? you think. But then something crests in the whitecaps beyond the spotlight.

"Is that your sea serpent?" Stavros calls out.

It's hard to tell from this distance. But capturing *any* footage of the large creature will be enough to entice the cryptid community. When you check the camera later, there is a brief moment when the creature is caught in the light. Is it enough to prove the existence of the legendary sea serpent? You hope so!

THE END

To read another adventure, turn to page 11.
To learn more about sea serpents, turn to page 103.

You decide to go to the upper deck. You hope to get better video of the creature up there. You detach the camera from the tripod and hang the strap around your neck. Then you climb the small ladder that leads to the upper area of the boat.

"Be careful up there!" Stavros calls out from below you. The sea has grown rough, and waves are crashing against the boat's side.

The risk is worth it, though. The upper deck provides a much better view. You should be able to get a clear shot of the creature from up here.

Click! Ca-click!

You eagerly take photos as the dark shape swims around the front of the boat. But just as the creature draws close, a large wave strikes the boat and sends you off-balance. The camera slips from your hands and lands in the water.

"Oh no!" You descend the ladder quickly. Stavros saw what happened and is acting fast. He grabs a net from the boat's deck and fishes the waterproof camera from the sea before it sinks.

"Thank you," you say, checking the footage you've captured.

The pictures are too grainy and blurry to make out anything clearly. But they're still enough to show that something very mysterious lives in the ocean.

THE END

To read another adventure, turn to page 11.
To learn more about sea serpents, turn to page 103.

The small deck above the helm could hold you. But the waves are getting rougher, and night is upon you. You don't want to risk it. You stay on the main deck with your camera. You should still get some good footage of the sea creature.

It seems to have disappeared, though. You swing the spotlight around, but you find only choppy waves.

SPLASH!

Something breaches the water right in front of you. It's hard to see what it is, though. You lean over to get a better look. As you do, a large fish leaps out of the water, right at you!

"Ahh!" you holler, completely taken by surprise.

The shock makes you stumble backward. You crash into the tripod that holds your camera. It topples over the railing and splashes into the sea.

"No!" you cry out, lunging after it.

But you lunge too far and fall over the railing. You land in the cold, choppy water and immediately begin flailing your arms.

"Help!" you cry out.

Stavros hurries along the deck, grabbing a life preserver. But before he can throw it to you, you feel something graze against your legs. Is it the shape from earlier? It certainly seems large enough!

You try to reach out for the camera, but it's too far away. Grudgingly, you grab the life preserver as your camera sinks beneath the waves. You choose to live over completing your mission.

THE END

To read another adventure, turn to page 11.
To learn more about sea serpents, turn to page 103.

"Should I pursue it?" Stavros asks again.

You look out at the waters, which have grown choppy. Then you shake your head. "Let's stay here," you suggest, hoping the shape slithering through the water will turn back toward you.

You keep an eye on it as the sun dips below the horizon and night falls. Stavros does his best to fight the waves. They crash against the side of the boat, spraying water up at you.

The shape seems to have disappeared, and you're beginning to feel dejected.

But then the creature reappears. A spiky hump breaches the surface near you. You're not quick enough to snap any photos this time. But you prepare for it to show up again.

Stavros appears next to you. "Should we try to slay the beast?" he asks.

"What do you mean?"

Stavros points to the side of the boat, where a harpoon cannon is mounted. Do you want to keep trying to take photos of the beast? Or would it be best to actually kill it?

Harpoon cannons launch barbed spears to kill whales or other large ocean creatures.

To use the harpoon, turn to page 68.
To keep trying to take photos, turn to page 70.

You traveled all this way to find proof of a cryptid. There's a good chance that one is swimming beneath you right now. Catching it would be a big triumph. But it's just the two of you on the boat. Will you even be able to pull the beast onto the boat if you do catch it?

You decide it's worth taking the chance. You nod. "Let's try to catch it!"

Stavros bustles along the deck as you fire up the spotlight near the boat's edge. He readies the harpoon.

With no one manning the helm, the boat rocks back and forth. The choppy waters have grown rougher, and it's hard to maintain your balance.

"There!" You swing the spotlight over and spy the shape near the starboard side of the boat. It's near, and Stavros swings the harpoon toward it.

The shape crashes against the side of the boat. Stavros stumbles just as he fires the harpoon.

THWACK!

Stavros's shot has gone astray, and the harpoon bolt punctures your leg!

"Aaghh!" you cry out, as pain courses through your body.

"Oh no, friend!" Stavros races over as you fall to the deck in agony. "We must get you to a medic! Quickly!"

Blackness overtakes you as you pass out from the pain. The last thing you think is that you should have stuck with shooting photos, instead of shooting harpoons at the beast.

THE END

To read another adventure, turn to page 11.
To learn more about sea serpents, turn to page 103.

"Well?" Stavros again nods in the direction of the harpoon. "How badly would you like to capture the creature?"

You consider it, but you have no desire to harm the creature. Plus, the waves are crashing against the hull of the boat. Aiming a harpoon could be a dangerous situation.

You shake your head. "Let's stick with shooting video, Stavros, and not the beast."

"As you say."

Stavros returns to the helm and steers the boat in the direction you last saw the shape.

As you continue scanning with the spotlight, you soon spy the large shape in the water again. You begin to record as it swims near the starboard side.

The creature never truly surfaces to reveal what it is. But you're determined to get it on video. Whether it's an oarfish or a legendary sea serpent, at least you'll have evidence.

After a time, the shape disappears into the depths of the sea. You're thrilled. In spite of the rough waves and the boat's constant rocking, you've captured footage of something special. What it is will be guessed at for years to come.

You and Stavros steer for shore. Your mission is a success!

THE END

To read another adventure, turn to page 11.
To learn more about sea serpents, turn to page 103.

Megalodon lived between 2 and 15 million years ago. Some scientists believe the giant shark could grow up to 80 feet (24 m) long.

CHAPTER 4

THE MIGHTY MEGALODON

An expedition to find the kraken or a sea serpent sounds interesting. But the possibility of finding a megalodon has captured your imagination.

Known as history's largest shark, the *Carcharocles megalodon,* or "giant tooth," prowled the oceans millions of years ago. It's believed that the monstrous creatures were between 60 and 80 feet (18 and 24 meters) long. Their teeth were three times bigger than a modern great white shark's.

It's hard to say when the massive beast went extinct. Scientists believe that megalodon died out well before humans evolved more than 2 million years ago.

Turn the page.

It's highly unlikely that the team of shark trackers saw something as big as a megalodon. But you want to see for yourself.

Looks like you're off to China!

You book a plane ticket and contact the shark team to let them know you'll be joining them. The woman in charge of the team, Lan Li, says she'll meet you at the harbor when you arrive.

"Were you among those who saw the large shark?" you ask her over the phone.

"I was," Lan replies. "We were near the Mariana Trench, studying tiger sharks. We're heading back to that region again. We'll wait for your arrival."

"Thank you. I'll see you in a few days."

The Mariana Trench is the deepest part of the ocean. The bottom is more than 36,000 feet (10,900 m) deep. It's the most likely place for something new and exciting to be discovered.

Your travels take you through the bustling city of Hong Kong to a smaller port city where Lan Li's team is based. When you arrive, you're surprised by the large size of the team's ship. They're well prepared for their work.

Research vessels are equipped with submersibles and a lot of high-tech gear to study the world's oceans.

Turn the page.

As you cross the dock toward the ship, a woman with short black hair slides down a ladder and approaches you.

"You must be the one who called about the shark," she states, holding out her hand. "I'm Lan Li. It's good to meet you."

You introduce yourself. Lan then gestures at the ship. "Welcome aboard," she says.

The ship launches a few hours later, taking you and the crew out to sea. Two days later, you reach your destination. After the ship drops anchor, Lan Li shows you their shark safety cage.

"You're free to use our safety cage, if you wish," she says.

You debate if the cage would be the best way to capture images of the large shark.

To use the cage, go to page 77.
To remain on the ship, turn to page 86.

"I think the cage will be a great way to see what's down there," you tell Lan.

While the crew prepares the large metal cage, you change into the wet suit you brought along. Lan's team has an oxygen tank, regulator, and mask for you to use.

When you're dressed, you get out your underwater camera. Then you climb into the cage.

"This is the area where we were tagging tiger sharks," Lan explains. "The chance of other sharks, like great whites, being present is fairly high. Are you ready?"

You nod and put in the oxygen mouthpiece. The team helps you into the cage, secures you, and gives you a thumbs-up.

You are lowered into the crystal-blue water of the ocean. It takes time for the cage to rattle and shake its way under the water.

Turn the page.

When you're finally beneath the surface, you're amazed at the clearness of the water and how easy it is to see.

You're lowered a long way down until you can see the ocean floor. The water is teeming with sea life. Fish swim in schools, darting back and forth along a rocky reef. Several tiger sharks like the ones the team was tracking are nearby as well.

You shoot photos and some video footage of it all. But as you do, a large shadow appears above you.

It's a great white shark.

It's nowhere near the size of a megalodon, but it's still a huge and dangerous creature. It swims around the cage as if to size you up. You raise your camera and shoot images of the shark. It's beautiful and sleek.

Even when inside a protective cage, divers need to be cautious with great white sharks. They can grow up to 20 feet (6 m) long.

But the great white turns out to be aggressive. It slams against the cage multiple times, causing you to lose your balance. You feel your camera slip from your hands. It drops through the cage bars and sinks to the ocean floor.

If you plan on getting any more footage, you have to go after it. But is it safe?

To go after the camera, turn to page 80.
To stay in the cage, turn to page 93.

You need to go after your camera, but there's no way you're going out there with the aggressive shark circling the cage. Instead, you wait patiently until it swims off into the distance.

You carefully unlatch the cage and swim out of it. You feel some fear, knowing that the great white could still return, but you need your camera. It's a chance you're willing to take. You swiftly swim toward the ocean floor in search of the camera.

There is a long, winding reef below you. Fish dart in and out of its gaps. You even see an octopus skirting and skimming along the ocean floor. It kicks up dirt and silt in its wake.

It takes you some time, but you finally spy your camera caught in the reef. Relieved, you swim over to free it.

Colorful coral reefs are home to a wide range of ocean life.

You're also feeling safer about being outside the cage. You take a moment to look around and snap photos of your surroundings. Looking in both directions, you can see the reef to your left growing larger. But there is also a trench in the ocean floor to your right. Either could offer a chance at finding something interesting.

To head left toward the reef, turn to page 82.
To head right toward the trench, turn to page 83.

You decide to head for the larger section of the reef. Swimming confidently, you make it there easily. You find that it's large enough for you to swim between the gaps.

As you do, though, a shadow once again appears. Before you know it, the great white shark you saw earlier darts out of the reef. Its jaws are open wide. You try to retreat, but you're caught up in the reef!

The angry shark is upon you, and there's no escape. Your search for the megalodon is over at the bottom of the ocean.

THE END

To read another adventure, turn to page 11.
To learn more about the megalodon, turn to page 103.

The reef was the last area you saw the great white shark. Exploring there doesn't seem like the best option. However, the trench looks like a great place to find something as large as a megalodon.

As you swim toward the trench, you see that it's larger than you thought at first. That's exciting. But it's also somewhat scary. Who knows what might be lurking down there? You begin to swim down into the depths of the trench. The light fades fast, so you click on small lamps on your scuba gear and your camera.

The trench is dark, yet beautiful. You begin recording video on your camera. Eventually you see the bottom of the trench. It's teeming with marine life swimming about. You see strange fish, jellyfish, squid, and other creatures. You sweep your camera around to get footage of all of it.

Turn the page.

It's beautiful. But it's not what you're searching for. You begin to get frustrated by the lack of something spectacular. Just as you're about to give up and swim back, a large shadow passes over you. Startled, you quickly look up to see what it is.

The light from your lamps is low. But you need to get photos of the creature.

Your heartbeat quickens. The creature's silhouette appears like a great white. But it's larger

than the one you saw before. You try to remain calm and aim your camera at the beast. You capture a fair amount of video before it swims off.

After a time, you swim out of the trench and head back to the ship. You pass the open cage and break the surface.

"Welcome back!" Lan says as you climb aboard the ship. "How was your hunt?"

"See for yourself!" The crew gathers around as you show off the video and photos. The images are dark, and it's hard to determine the size of the shape. But you feel confident in your discovery. Was it the supposedly extinct megalodon? You don't know. But whatever it was, it was massive.

THE END

To read another adventure, turn to page 11.
To learn more about the megalodon, turn to page 103.

Going down in the cage could provide a great view of the megalodon if it appeared. But you know that even the strong cage would be little protection against such a huge and powerful creature. You shake your head.

"I think I'll stay dry for now," you tell Lan.

"Suit yourself," she replies. "It's there if you need it. And we have scuba gear for you, as well."

You find a good place near the bow of the ship to set up your tripod.

Hours later, you've seen nothing.

The day passes, and the team observes any underwater activity using their sonar equipment. You knew that coming all this way to find a long-extinct creature would be a long shot. But you had to try.

Then, as dusk approaches, something huge breaches the surface of the water in the distance.

"Did you see that?" one of the crew members calls out.

"I did!" Lan replies.

"Me too!" you excitedly add.

"It's far bigger than the tiger sharks we've been tracking," Lan says. "Let's see if we can get a little closer."

You agree. You already started recording video of the beast as it slips in and out of sight. But you want to get a better view. This could be your only chance.

You quickly don your scuba wet suit. "Help me with the rest," you tell the crew. They hurry to outfit you with a tank of oxygen, a regulator for your mouth, and a pair of goggles.

You grab your camera and splash into the water. It's cold and brisk, and even in the wet suit, it takes your breath away.

Turn the page.

You can't believe you're throwing caution to the wind, but you don't want to miss this chance. You swim closer to the shape in the water. However, as you get closer, you notice the creature isn't alone.

A great white shark is also circling the area!

To swim back to the ship, go to page 89.
To defend yourself from the shark, turn to page 90.

Great white sharks often have more than 50 razor-sharp teeth!

Frantically, you swim back toward the ship. But you've gotten too close. The shark begins to swim your way!

You've been around great whites before. You know humans aren't part of their usual diet. But this one seems overly aggressive. The great white is on you before you can reach the ship. Pain sears through your leg as the beast chomps down hard. The water around you turns red with blood.

"Help!" you cry out.

The ship's crew throws out a life preserver to pull you close to the ship. You feel the shark release your leg, and the crew quickly drags you aboard.

"Thank . . . you . . ." is all you can say before you pass out. Your hunt for the megalodon is over.

THE END

To read another adventure, turn to page 11.
To learn more about the megalodon, turn to page 103.

The shark hasn't noticed you yet. You know enough not to panic. You've been in the ocean with many dangerous creatures before. You know how to defend yourself if necessary.

It looks like that may be the case now. The shark turns in the water and heads in your direction.

Great white sharks don't typically eat humans. They prefer fish and other marine life. But they're also the most aggressive predator in the ocean. You know they can be dangerous.

The shark continues swimming in your direction. Your heart thuds in your chest. You grip the camera hard, preparing to stand your ground. When the shark is close enough, you'll be ready to swing your camera hard at its sensitive gills, nose, or eyes.

THWACK!

You've startled the shark. It swims away. But then it circles around and comes at you from another angle.

You twist in the water. As the shark nears again, you smack it hard on the gills again.

THWACK!

This time, the great white is so startled that it turns and swims away.

You remain where you are, treading water and waiting to see if the shark will return.

It does not.

You stay in place in the water. You wait to see if the creature you spied earlier will make another appearance.

There! To your left, the mighty ocean beast breaks the surface. You raise your camera and quickly snap photos of it.

Turn the page.

Then you dive beneath the surface and capture images of it underwater as well. However, the creature is some distance away. And the growing darkness has made it less visible underwater. But it doesn't matter. You're excited about the images you're capturing.

When you're safely back aboard the ship, you scan the footage. Yes! You've got something! The images are dark and moody. But there's definitely a shadowy figure in them. It's far too enormous to be a great white shark. Is it a megalodon? You can't be sure. But you're convinced it's definitely *something* not normally seen in the ocean.

THE END

To read another adventure, turn to page 11.
To learn more about the megalodon, turn to page 103.

You watch as your camera floats away, down and out of sight. The great white remains alongside the cage, rubbing against it. It's not safe to exit the cage. Not yet.

You remain inside the cage where it's safe. Eventually the great white swims away. But you're running out of oxygen, and it's beginning to grow dark. You signal the crew on the ship to bring you back up.

The cage rattles, and you begin to rise back to the surface. The crew cranks the cage up beside the ship and hauls it in.

"I lost my camera," you explain to Lan. "If there's another tank of oxygen, I need to go retrieve it."

Lan places her hands on her hips. "We have more tanks," she says. "But is it safe enough to go back down?"

Turn the page.

"I can get it," you assure her.

Lan looks doubtful, but she asks a crew member to grab a reserve tank of oxygen. He equips you with it, and you dive backward off the ship into the water.

You swim down toward the ocean floor. Because of the dimming light, you click on a small lamp on your wet suit. Soon, you can see a large reef running along the ocean floor. It's most likely where your camera landed. But the ocean floor is immense. Your camera could be lost anywhere among the silt and dirt stirred up by sea creatures.

Where should you search?

To search the reef, go to page 95.
To search the ocean floor, turn to page 98.

The reef is huge and filled with large gaps. It's most likely the place where your camera came to rest.

You swim down toward the reef, noticing all of the sea life. Schools of fish swarm around you, caught in the lamp light of your wet suit. But there's no sign of your camera yet.

Then you spot a glint of reflected light and swim toward it. Sure enough, the camera strap is caught on some coral, and your camera is hanging from it.

Thank goodness, you think, retrieving the camera from the reef.

With camera in hand, you prepare to swim toward the surface. But then something catches your eye. It's nearly buried in the silt on the ocean floor.

Turn the page.

You reach out and pluck it from the dirt. It's a tooth! And not just any tooth—it's huge. It's even bigger than a great white shark's tooth.

You realize what you have found and grow excited. You quickly swim to the surface with your find.

"Did you find your camera?" Lan asks as you climb the ladder back onto the ship.

"That and more!"

You strip off the scuba gear and set your camera aside.

"Look at this!" You pull out the huge tooth and show it to Lan.

She runs it between her fingers and whistles. "This is much larger than a tiger shark," she says. "Even the samples of great white teeth we have are not this big. This is quite a find!"

The only known physical evidence of megalodon are fossilized teeth. The giant shark's teeth grew up to 7 inches (18 centimeters) long!

You're incredibly excited by your find. It may not be as huge as a megalodon tooth. But it's proof that something massive is prowling the waters of the Pacific Ocean!

THE END

To read another adventure, turn to page 11.
To learn more about the megalodon, turn to page 103.

You quickly scan the reef area. But you feel like your camera would have fallen to the ocean floor. You're worried that if it did fall there, then there's a chance it'll be buried before you find it.

You swim away from the reef and head to the open ocean floor. Sea life skims about, and a school of colorful fish circles you. The light from your lamp is low, making it hard to see much. A squid whisks its way past you.

As you scan the ocean floor, you spy a trench to your right. The trench could be where your camera drifted. It could also be very deep. Your search just became more difficult. But you need to at least try to see if the camera is down there.

You swim to the trench and dive down into it. It's dark and hard to see. It doesn't take you long to realize that your camera is gone. There's no way you'll find it in the murky trench.

Little is known about deep, dark ocean trenches. Could a giant, ancient beast like megalodon lurk in them?

Dejected, you swim up out of the trench. As you head back toward the surface, you spy something in the water.

No. Not something. Some *things*.

Sharks. A whole group, or shiver, of them. Great whites. And they look hungry.

You need to hide.

To hide in the reef, turn to page 100.
To hide in the trench, turn to page 101.

You race toward the reef. Perhaps you can hide in one of the gaps there until the sharks are gone.

Fortunately, the great whites don't stay long. They swim away in search of prey elsewhere. As you swim out of your hiding place, something catches your eye.

Looking closer, you see it's a tooth! And it's not just any tooth. It's much larger than any you've seen before. It could be a tooth from a great white shark. But you've seen those before, and this is much bigger.

You aren't sure what you've found. The tooth may not be as huge as a megalodon tooth. But it proves that something incredibly big, and maybe incredibly deadly, is prowling the waters of the Pacific Ocean!

THE END

To read another adventure, turn to page 11.
To learn more about the megalodon, turn to page 103.

One of the great whites starts swimming in your direction. As it draws near, you dive back into the trench to hide.

You click off your lamp and wait in the darkness for the shark to pass. But it doesn't leave. Instead it circles above you as if lying in wait. You look below for a way to escape. But then you see another group of sharks coming up out of the trench—straight for you!

You know the sharks are unlikely to attack, but you don't want to risk it. You swim as quickly as you can out of the trench and head to the surface.

When you reach the ship, you quickly climb the ladder. You're safe. But your camera is lost along with your photos and video. Your mission to find the megalodon has ended in failure.

THE END

To read another adventure, turn to page 11.
To learn more about the megalodon, turn to page 103.

Ancient sailors were often terrified that a giant kraken or other sea monster might destroy their ships while at sea.

CHAPTER 5

SEA MONSTERS: REAL OR EXTINCT?

Earth's oceans have long been a source of mystery and wonder. What could be hiding in the depths? Ancient myths and legends about giant, powerful creatures like the kraken only added to this sense of wonder.

In Nordic folklore, the kraken haunted the seas around Norway, Iceland, and Greenland. Sailors often told stories about how the beast could wrap its tentacles around a ship and pull it under while swallowing the ship's crew whole.

But was there ever a real kraken?

The closest creature to a kraken we know of was discovered in 1853. That year a giant squid was found on a beach in Denmark.

The dead creature proved that what ancient sailors had seen while at sea was likely an enormous squid or octopus. However, the legend of the kraken still captures people's imaginations today.

Much like the kraken, the sea serpent has its roots in ancient mythology. Some legends describe it as being like a dragon. In other tales the beast resembles a giant snake living in the ocean depths.

But what were sailors truly seeing?

Legends about sea serpents have been around for hundreds of years. But no animal has ever been captured to prove its existence. The sea creature most likely mistaken for sea serpents is the oarfish.

Oarfish are huge fish with long, snakelike bodies. They can grow to more than 50 feet (15 m) long. They usually live deep in the ocean. Oarfish are rarely seen, and little is known about them. But with their long, curving bodies, it's easy to see how they might be thought of as sea serpents.

The megalodon was the largest shark to ever roam the ocean. The kraken and sea serpent have their roots in mythology. But the megalodon was a real animal that lived millions of years ago.

The only megalodon fossils found are of the beast's teeth. They are prized among fossil hunters for their jagged edges and enormous size.

Most megalodon teeth are dated between 15.9 million and 2.6 million years ago. Scientists aren't sure exactly when the megalodon became extinct. But by studying the beast's teeth, they believe the shark could grow up to an amazing 80 feet (24 m) long!

When it comes to ancient sea monsters, even the mighty kraken would likely not survive an encounter with the giant megalodon!

Sea Monsters Around the World

Sailors have reported seeing strange ocean creatures and sea monsters for hundreds of years. Many of these monsters were likely real creatures that sailors didn't know about or recognize. Still, the world's oceans and deep lakes hold many mysteries. Who knows what sorts of creatures are yet to be discovered?

Kraken (Norway):

The fearsome kraken was said to pull large ships under the ocean and eat entire crews. The legends were likely based on giant squid, which can grow to about 40 feet (12 m) long.

Megalodon (Pacific Ocean):

The megalodon was one of the most fearsome creatures to have ever lived. The giant shark's teeth measured up to 7 inches (18 cm) long. Based on this, scientists think the beast grew up to 80 feet (24 m) long. That's almost three times as large as a modern-day great white shark!

St. Augustine Monster (Florida):

In 1896, a huge mass of decaying flesh was discovered on the beach in St. Augustine, Florida. For many years it was thought to be a dead giant octopus. Scientists later determined that the fleshy glob was the remains of a whale.

Sea Serpents (Worldwide):

Tales of huge, snakelike sea serpents that attack ships come from all over the world. Stories about these monsters are probably based on oarfish, which can grow 50 feet (15 m) long or more.

Montauk Monster (New York):

The body of a strange, hairless creature was discovered on the beach near Montauk, New York, in 2008. At first people wondered if it was an unidentified sea creature. But researchers believe the beast was a dead raccoon or dog that had lost its hair and was partially decayed.

Bunyip (Australia):

Native Australians have long told tales of the legendary bunyip. The creature is said to resemble a seal with a head like a bulldog. It's believed that stories of these mythical creatures are based on seals that sometimes find their way up Australia's rivers.

Glossary

bioluminescence (bye-oh-loo-muh-NEH-suhns)—light produced by living organisms

breach (BREECH)—to emerge from or jump out of the water

cephalopod (SEF-uh-luh-pod)—a type of mollusk, such as an octopus or squid, that lives in the ocean and has tentacles and a beak

cryptid (KRIP-tihd)—an animal or creature that people have claimed to see but has never been proven to exist

cryptozoology (krip-toh-zoh-AH-luh-jee)—the study of evidence for unproven creatures such as Bigfoot or the Loch Ness monster

extinct (ik-STINGKT)—no longer living; an extinct animal is one that has died out, with no more of its kind

galley (GAL-ee)—a small kitchen, often found on a ship, plane, or camper

helm (HELM)—the part of a ship or boat by which it is steered and navigated

port (PORT)—the left side of a ship as you look forward

reef (REEF)—an underwater strip of rocks, coral, or sand near the surface of the ocean

shiver (SHIV-uhr)—a group of sharks

silhouette (sih-luh-WET)—the outline of something that shows its shape

simulate (SIM-yuh-layt)—to copy or imitate the appearance or actions of something

silt (SILT)—small particles of soil that settle at the bottom of a river, lake, or ocean

sonar (SOH-nar)—a device that uses sound waves to find underwater objects; sonar stands for sound navigation and ranging

starboard (STAR-bohrd)—the right side of a ship as you look forward

tentacle (TEN-tuh-kuhl)—a long, armlike body part some animals use to touch, grab, or smell

Other Paths to Explore

>>> Look at the descriptions of creatures on pages 106–107. Reports of strange ocean creatures can be found all over the world. If you could pick one unexplained beast to track down, which would it be? How would you prepare for your journey? Where do you think your search would begin?

>>> Scientists believe there are many undiscovered animal species in the world's oceans. Think about the deep ocean trench you see during the hunt for megalodon. What other kinds of creatures do you think might live at such depths? What do you think life looks like thousands of feet below the ocean's surface?

>>> During your adventures, you relied on cameras to take photos and capture video evidence of the creatures you were investigating. What other kinds of evidence could you look for instead? Could you try to get audio recordings or use a different kind of camera? What if a body was discovered? How would you determine if it was one of the legendary creatures you were studying?

Read More

Goddu, Krystyna Poray. *Sea Monsters: From Kraken to Nessie*. Minneapolis: Lerner, 2017.

Polinsky, Paige V. *Giant Squid: Mysterious Monster of the Deep*. Minneapolis: Abdo Publishing, 2017.

Internet Sites

Animals in Sea History: Oarfish
seahistory.org/sea-history-for-kids/oarfish-harmless-fish-or-deadly-sea-serpent/

What Was the Kraken?
wonderopolis.org/wonder/what-was-the-kraken

 **Brandon Terrell** (B.1978 – D.2021) Brandon was a passionate reader and Star Wars fan, amazing father, son, uncle, friend, and devoted husband. Brandon received his undergraduate degree from the Minneapolis College of Art and Design and his Master of Fine Arts in Writing for Children and Young Adults from Hamline University in St. Paul, MN. Brandon was a talented storyteller, authoring more than 100 books for children in his career. This book is dedicated in his memory.—Happy Reading!

Index